Already over 50 5star
Seren~~ity series.~~

5 ***** Reviews from Book 1, The Island of Survival

"What a beautiful romantic story"

"Wonderfully insightful and compelling to read, this is a book that is hard to put down...!"

"A New Paulo Coelho"

The author displays a three-fold gift; that of a story-teller, the ability to create a powerful parable and the elusive capacity to present genuine and unsentimental paths towards self-healing.

This is the tale of Faron, a man who wishes to commit suicide at the age of 40 after a life that, on the surface, seems laden with disasters. His soul's/self's subsequent journey towards self-understanding and, thus, healing is the warp and weft of this book, the first in a series. But this is no depressive book; it bears comparison with the ultimate uplift of 'Veronica Decides to Die' by Paulo Coelho.

This book is brief, yet its brevity has a purpose; Gedall strips away the palaver and preachiness of so much self-help literature and replaces it with a simple tale, simply told, to which the reader can bring his/her self, unencumbered by the voice of a whispering martinet.

This is, in short, a beautiful, revolutionary and revelatory work."

"This book was a book that really took me on an adventure. I bought it because I was looking for a cliff hanger to take my mind away from the stress that was going on at work. It was exactly what I was looking for."

"I really have never read anything like this before, and it is transfixing in the way that the author cleverly brings to life a story, … it offers insights and wisdoms into the psyche which are revelatory."

"The story transmitted me to familiar places I haven't been to. Well-polished story. The author is undeniably extraordinary."

"… It explores the background of the main character in a very insightful way. We are all products of our past, that much is true, and I enjoyed reading about his French aristocratic mother and distant alcoholic father.

When Faron commits suicide at age 40 (we don't get to know any details as to the exact reasons- just that he has hurt a lot of people, but undoubtedly more will be explained later on in the series) he is transported to the first island called Survival.

In a prehistoric time as a creature in between ape and man he gets to do just that with people he knew from his own modern times. He experiences all facets of survival in a very down to earth human way".

The Island of Serenity

Book 1

Survival

Gary Edward Gedall
23/11/2014

Published by

From Words to Worlds,

Lausanne, Switzerland

www.fromwordstoworlds.com

ISBN: **2-940535-12-5**
ISBN 13: **978-2-940535-12-5**

About the Author

Gary Edward Gedall is a state registered psychologist, psychotherapist, trained in Ericksonian hypnosis and EMDR.

He has ordinary and master's degrees in Psychology from the Universities of Geneva and Lausanne and an Honours Degree in Management Sciences from Aston University in the UK.

He has lived as an associate member of the Findhorn Spiritual Community, has been a regular visitor to the Osho meditation centre in Puna, India. And as part of his continuing quest into alternative beliefs and healing practices, he completed the three-year practical training, given by the Foundation for Shamanic Studies in 2012.

He is now, (2014 – 2016), studying for a DAS, (Diploma of Advanced Studies), as a therapist using horses.

Quora Best Writer of the Year 2015

His hobbies are; writing, western riding and spoiling his children.

He is currently living and working in Lausanne, Switzerland.

Realization, Repentance, Redemption, Release & Rebirth

This book was inspired by the realization that I had never really mourned the death of my older brother, Lloyd, to whom this series is dedicated.

In my therapy practice, I am all too often confronted with patients who feel that their lives no longer have any sense or perspective. It is my job to help them find back the sense of their lives, and to encourage them in finding again some optimism that things can get better.

This book is for all of you that have made errors, mistakes, stupid and destructive choices and actions, (which should cover approximatively 99% of the world's population).

We have all got it wrong sometimes in our lives, but it is never too late to start to get it right.

Remember, you can always find teachers; therapists, spiritual and religious guides, etc., etc,. who are there to help you on your path.

If you need help, don't hesitate to reach out, you don't have to face your demons alone.

I take also this opportunity to thank my daughter, Kyra for her help in the structuring of the series, and the time and interest that she invested in reflecting with me on the stories.

By the same Author

Adventures with the Master

REMEMBER

Tasty Bites (Series – published or in preproduction)
Face to Face
Free 2 Luv
Heresy
Love you to death
Master of all Masters
Pandora's Box
Shame of a family
The Noble Princess
The Ugly Barren Fruit Tree
The Woman of my Dreams

The Island of Serenity, Pt 1 Destruction

(Series – published or in preproduction)

Book1 :	**The Island of Survival**
Book 2:	**Sun & Rain**
Book 3:	**Pleasure**
Book 4:	**Rise & Fall**
Book 5:	**Esteem**
Book 6:	**The Faron Show**

(Non Fiction)	*The Zen approach to Low Impact Training and Sports*
	Picturing the Mind

Disclaimer:

The characters and events related in my books are a synthesis of all that I have seen and done, the people that I have met and their stories. Hence, there are events and people that have echoes with real people and real events, however no character is taken purely from any one person and is in no way intended to depict any person, living or dead.

Contents

1. Sorry

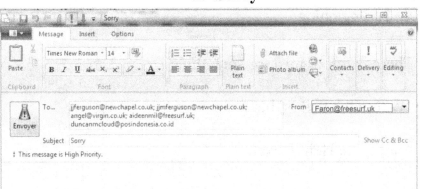

To... jjferguson@newchapel.co.uk; jjmferguson@newchapel.co.uk; angel@virgin.co.uk; aideenmil@freesurf.uk; duncanmcloud@posindonesia.co.id

From Faron@freesurf.uk

Subject Sorry

! This message is High Priority.

By the time you are reading this, I will be dead.

Tomorrow was to be my fortieth birthday, I just couldn't face it, so like the coward that I am, I am copping out from that too.

I know that I have screwed up your lives, as well as my own, and I am sorry, but it wasn't really my fault. You see, we are all but the product of our pasts. None of you know all of my story; so, once and for all, I am going to write it all down.

You might well be shocked by what you are going to read, but before I go, I need to get this off of my chest.

It is not a glorious story, I've done some shitty things, I know, but I never set out to be a bad person.

This is my story .....

2. Beginning

There is fog or mist, or something.

"Where the hell is this?"

"Not quite Hell, Faron."

"Who are you, where are you, how do you know my name?"

"Who I am is of no importance; where I am, is not here and I know your name because I am here to help you."

"But where am I, am I dead?"

"You are in-between."

"In-between what?"

"Here and there."

"Is this purgatory?"

"You might choose to call it that."

"Why am I here?"

"Why do you think?"

"Because you don't know where to send me?"

"Where you should go next, will have to be decided."

"But I can't change what I've done."

"You can change who you are now."

"But it's too late."

"If it was too late, there would be no point in you being here."

"Listen, whoever or whatever you are, it is too late, I've totally screwed up my life, there's no point in trying to change anything."

"Fine, then I hope that you like this scenery,…"

"There is no scenery, just clouds or fog."

"… because this is where you will stay."

"For how long?"

"Until you accept to change."

"That's my choice, change or stay?"

"Isn't it the only choice, to change, or stay the same?"

"To change or remain the same?"

"Change or remain the same."

"Okay, change it is."

"Change it is."

"Okay."

Early Years

3. My royal lineage

Some children are born with a silver spoon in their mouths, I was born with one rammed up my arse.

That way I could; sit up straight, stand up straight and shine from within.

My mother was the direct descendent from an obscure French noble family, who had the good idea to take an extended vacation, with their English neighbours, so they could keep their heads, when all about them were losing theirs.

They arrived in England, with very little else other than their nobility and a small box of very expensive jewellery.

They bought a smallish house in the South; the Duke found work as a private tutor and the Duchess as a humble seamstress.

Their children were brought up as aristocrats in exile; all the virtues of the off-springs 'de bonne famille' were drilled into them, in anticipation for the day when they would return to reclaim their rightful heritage..

Through the generations, the myth of their nobility was passed down, as was an education of the highest standards.Ttheir impeccable manners and values being the best compensation against the loss of everything else.

Of course they had the obvious obligation to keep up appearances. Never must they be seen in public unless they were perfectly attired, with clean and appropriate clothing, hair and make-up faultlessly applied, males and females, alike.

The concept of 'fur coat and no knickers', comes all too easily to mind. No matter what they might have to deprive themselves of in the privacy of their own homes, just as long as the public image was impeccable, all was well with the world.

The family rules about the jewels that they succeeded to bring over, is a case in point.

One would have thought that the first thing that they would have to do, would be to sell off the stuff, so as to be able to afford a more comfortable lifestyle.

In fact, the choice was just the opposite, they sold off as few as possible, just enough to purchase their little house, and to keep them fed until the Duke succeeded to land his first job.

The jewels, not only had value as family heirlooms but were intrinsically linked to their projected image. To protect this choice for future generations, the Duke placed all the jewels in a form of permanent trust. The female family members were allowed to keep and wear them, but without any legal title, so could never sell them.

The jewels were then passed down to their female descendants, with the logical caveat that if they had no female descendants, of their own they would be passed on to the closest female relative.

This small detail had some rather important ramifications on our family relationships, creating the imperative need to have at least one surviving female offspring in each family.

Such a tradition would certainly have been of benefit in many of the more Eastern countries.

Slowly but surely, the family clawed its way back up the social ladder; the men were noticed for their bravery and honour and graded during the wars.

One family legend has it that during the First World War, many of the soldiers were complaining about the food and conditions in the trenches. My grand or great grand uncle suddenly decided to appear one evening, to take his evening 'meal', correctly 'dressed for dinner'.

Unfortunately, his brilliantly white shirt also attracted the attention of a sniper from the German camp, and, lacking a protective helmet, was cleanly shot through the side of his head.

He was known as being the most elegantly dressed casualty of the whole war.

The women were sort after by the sons of local landowners for their modesty and grace.

And as education became universally available, their impeccable breeding and intellectual investment naturally brought them to the top of the heap.

These successes did little to soften the importance of their 'nobles in exile' strict education; although, now, there was no longer the idea that they would return to France to recuperate their domain.

It seems that they had realised that their intrinsic family project of joining the most privileged of classes, could be fulfilled but with less effort, as they had found a much softer target.

As they were now moving into the higher echelons of British society, it became, if anything, more important that they integrate even deeper into the British aristocratic world.

And so my mother was born into the British lower nobility; Antoinette-Marie Claude Armitage.

She was the younger sister:

Geneviève-Hélène Marie was her 'ainée' by three years, and Antoinette suffered greatly from the long shadow cast by her pretty, charming and intellectually brilliant sister.

However, the strong, family directive of, 'onwards and upwards', was in no way lost in her, and she must have secretly vowed to scale the social ladder, faster and higher than her, otherwise unassailably successful sister.

To fulfil this self-imposed objective, there seemed to be only one path, a very good marital alliance. She would either have to marry a nobleman, already high up in the county's social circles, or someone quite rich, or at least on the way to so being.

As all the young, eligible, noble bachelors were already well sought after by many young, pretty and even, God-forbid, intelligent young ladies of impeccable backgrounds and heritage, Antoinette-Marie hedged her bets and set off to find a young, multi-millionaire in the making.

She found that man in my father, James John Ferguson.

4. My other Royal Linage

J.J. Ferguson, as he was known to everybody had also come from a type of royalty, as popular myth would have it. One of his direct ancestors was supposed to have been an illegitimate son of one of the King James's.

His mother, in a bizarre type of mirroring of the story of my mother's family, (which is so unlikely that it could only be true), fed the young bastard with stories of his true nobility and of how, at some future moment in history, he would regain his true, noble status.

This aristocratic, family heritage was passed on, from generation to generation, finally arriving at a miserable, terraced house, in the darkest streets of one of Glasgow's dormitories for its army of dockers.

J.J., like most of his generation was apprenticed into 'the works' and fought his way through to the end, to resurface some years later as a highly skilled engineer.

He could, of course, have stayed, as chose most of his compatriots, to live and work, in and around the family and friends that they had known all their lives.

However, J.J., nurtured with stories and promises of a stolen birth-right, knowing that he was destined for greater things, gathered his few belongings and headed down South, ready to retrieve his fame and fortune.

He, for no apparent reason, installed himself in a small engineering town, dependant on the company from which he was to start his mini empire. The company that he began working for as a simple factory hand was aptly named as 'New Chapel Engineering', since New Chapel was not surprisingly, the name of the town.

The poverty and hardship experienced by our Scottish neighbours, (speaking as one born and breed in the comfort of the English Southern countryside), over many generations, has produced a race, where survival has had to be fought for and hardworking is the lowest level of effort.

That said, when my father started working in an English factory, alongside the average English worker, it took hardly any time, (seven years, I believe), before he was promoted from simple worker to supervisor, to shop supervisor, to factory supervisor.

The other national trait, much attacked and much maligned, is that of thriftiness. J.J. was surely true to his Scottish heritage on that regard.

He lived as frugally as was humanly possible; where others of his level would buy themselves cars, fancy clothes, even houses, not to mention the money to seduce all manner of available women, J.J. scrimped and saved, schemed and plotted.

Unlike the family of my mother, J.J. had no need to keep up appearances, his nobility was his own affair. In fact, his secret was so well hidden, I doubt if anyone, ever, even in their wildest fantasies, suspected that beneath his rather rough Glaswegian exterior, there lurked the heart of the most noble of Scottish royalty.

All the time waiting for an opportunity; the hunter, patiently sitting on his rock, contemplating the horizon.

Confident that sooner or later, his prey, like an iron bar, to a charged electro-magnet, would be attracted to him, and then, with one, swift, sure stroke, it would be his.

The British economy seems somewhere to be heavily influenced by the fact that we are an island nation. Just as the tides can mount and parts of the country can find itself flooded, at other times, they recede so far away, that we can fear to be living in a desert, experiencing weeks of parching drought.

In much the same way, the economy has an unsettling habit of passing from boom to bust. Which is to say, that there are periods of wealth, inflation and optimism. Unfortunately, just around the financial corner, we find ourselves pitched into poverty, deflation and pessimism.

During one of these, 'up periods', the factory owner, imagining that the economy would continue to boom for some years to come, borrowed a vast sum of money to expand his factory and earn himself a fortune into the bargain.

Needless to say, the boom only lasted long enough for him to borrow and spend the money, before the economy stalled again, leaving him with a debt, so important, that he couldn't even manage to pay off the monthly interest. He had no choice but to file for bankruptcy.

Ten years of working and saving had built up a considerable sum of cash in my father's bank account and a great deal of confidence, in his seriousness and stability in the mind of his local bank manager.

It didn't take much time before his bank agreed to take over the factory's debts, and my father became, in his mid-thirties, one of the youngest factory owners ever.

By the age of forty, he had added three more factories to his growing empire and was well on his way to becoming a wealthy man.

And so it came about that the young apparent pauper, in the course of a few short years, succeeded to conquer the first territories, on his noble quest to regain his birth rite.

The prince had returned.

5. A Noble Union

It was around this time that my father started to appear at certain charity events.

It seems that my mother; true to her goal, had started to attend charity events some time before.

Comforted in the idea that only wealthy patrons, with nothing better to do with their money, would imagine to spend a small fortune, to assist at a luncheon or a dinner, which they could enjoy at a tenth of the price, at any decent restaurant in town.

J.J., from his side, although not looking for a wealthy partner, had more-than-likely reflected that, to find a suitable spouse, he would have to frequent the localities that women from those social levels might congregate.

As he was rarely if ever, invited to society balls and such, the obvious solution was to invite himself to charity luncheons and dinners.

It was surely my mother that would have made the first move, she was always the predator when it came to social advancement, J.J., was much too timid and shy in anything that wasn't to do with business and finances.

From what I later found out, the courtship was quite short and uneventful; my mother's family were of course totally against her marrying this, 'personne', this no-body, even if he had, had the unlikely chance to become financially comfortable.

On the other side; his family were just as antagonistic against these Franco-English snobs, full of airs and graces, who had never done a decent days work in their 'entire lives'.

This, of course, deterred my mother, not in the least.

She had, to some degree expected a certain resistance from her side of the family, and honestly preferred that his 'kin' would have the good grace, to keep as far away as humanly possible.

If she could have rebuilt Hadrian's Wall just for them, she wouldn't have hesitated for even a second.

What she did do was to organise a typical English, society wedding, reported in the Tattler, and organised by the chief buyer at Liberty's.

She then let it be known, through various channels that the wedding would, 'of course', be an intimate affaire and only limited to family, close friends and the most socially 'interesting' people of the year and then waited for the polite, indirect requests to arrive.

It was, so I have often heard, a resounding success, and that, if nothing else, was what was necessary, to launch my mother, finally, into the circles of highest society.

My father, for his part, took the next six months to recover financially, from this intimate affaire.

One could image, to install herself and to continue to circulate in these prominent circles might have led to financial ruin, but my mother was no fool, she was much too astute to risk killing the goose that laid the golden eggs.

If fact, when there were none of her 'people' to witness, she was very careful with money.

6.   Two more for the table

She agreed a monthly allowance with my father, (which of course increased over the years), which was to cover all the household expenses, (except the salary of the staff), mine, and later my brother's needs and the rest was for her.

Our day clothes were bought from reputable, but relatively inexpensive stores, our food was ordered from the local supermarket.

Our pocket money was no more than the other kids of our age, living in the same village. (In fact, I later learned that many received even more than we did).

When we would ask for a special toy or plaything or clothing; mother would often complain that she didn't have enough spare money that month.

And that we would have to wait until she had, unless we would wish to use some of our own pocket money or savings to pay for it ourselves.

It was only when I reached teenage years that I realised that she could decide, at any given moment, that some event that she was invited to, would need a new outfit, and in that case, money was always available, and not in short supply either.

Mother, of course didn't see herself as mean, only that money was not to be wasted, (that means on things that I or my brother might wish for), but was to be saved so that it could be used for important things, which meant to say, impressing people.

My father was not at all interested in how my mother saw fit to dispense with the money that he gave her, just as long as the house was clean, well stocked with food that he liked, and that they never ran out of that most essential Scottish commodity, good whiskey.

For you see, my father liked a tipple from time to time.

Over the years; that 'time to time' became less and less separated, until it became unusual not to see him with a large, diamond cut, whiskey glass in his hand and the smell of a single highland malt on his increasingly labouring breath.

Before I was born, my father had already sold off two of the factories that he had acquired before meeting my mother.

He had then re-invested the benefits to buy out two competing building companies, which he merged into one mega concern; hence, tactically sawing up all the major building contracts over three counties, for the foreseeable future, all in one elegant manoeuvre.

However, the company from which he had started his mini empire, 'New Chapel Engineering', was never to be sold. He had worked his way up from nothing, to becoming the owner of this smallish factory. He knew every nook and cranny of it, and almost every one of the workforce by name.

The year before I was born, the old manor house, once owned by the Earls of Drayford, until the last of the line died at 26, from an incurable case of syphilis, came onto the market, my father didn't hesitate even for one moment, before snapping it up.

It was the perfect object for both my parents to show off that they had reached their goals of returning to the rightful level, from which their ancestors had fallen.

7.   Marie Madeleine

As soon as my mother fell pregnant with me, she searched for and found a distant, poor, French relative, a sort of maiden aunt, to come over and live with us.

She was what they call a 'jeune fille au pair', although she was anything but a young girl, more than likely already in her late-forties or early fifties.

As a family member; plucked out of abject poverty, given a decent job, room, food, money, (actually not much more than pocket money really), my mother was confident that she would act in a serious and trustworthy manner.

In fact, Marie Madeleine did much more than that; she became a de facto mother substitute for me, caring for me, as she would if I had been the child that she never had.

This investment in me never wavered, even after the birth of my little brother Jean-Jacques Malcolm Ferguson two years and three months my junior.

It must be said that my earliest years were not unpleasant, with Marie Madeleine as my constant surveillant and Jean-Jacques who became more and more a playmate as the years progressed.

As to my parents I saw them mainly but in passing moments, we might cross my mother, ('Maman', as she preferred that we called her), in the morning, as we were preparing to go out somewhere.

'Bonjour mes chers, tout se passe bien?'

'Oui, Madame, tout va très bien. Et vous, Madame ?'

'Ça va, ça va, je suis très occupée. Soyez sages, mes enfants'.

'Oui, Maman.'

'Bonne journée.'

As you might probably have noticed, mother would speak to us in French, this was intentioned for us to acquire French as a mother tongue.

The choice to have imported Marie-Madeleine, who only spoke French, was clearly part of this particular project.

Fortunately for us; neither the cook, Alice, the maid, nor the woman that came twice weekly to do cleaning spoke any French, so we did also have the opportunity to hear and begin to speak some English as well.

8.   J.J. Made from Girders in Scotland

But what of our interactions with our father? J.J. very often worked very late during the week, mostly slept late both Saturday and Sunday mornings, (sleeping off the effects of too much Scotch the night before, I found out later on).

On Sunday afternoons he would go off to play golf on our local golf course, an act that gave him great pleasure and pride, after the rather problematical start of his relationship with the club….

When my father first moved to New Chapel, as a very lowly factory worker, there was nothing much for him to do at the weekend.

He didn't know anybody and he didn't give himself the right to go out drinking regularly, as he had already decided that he was going to save up for his 'great deal', (even though, at the time, he had absolutely no idea of what it could be).

However, as some people might not know, golf is a Scottish nation sport and there exists, in some parts of Scotland, the possibility for even those on quite miserable incomes, to become acquainted with it.

My father was one such person, in fact he was pretty good at it.

His keen eye and dogged perseverance, made that quite soon he was winning the small local tournaments, and his club was pushing him to risk entering for the more prestigious competitions.

Unfortunately, the entrance fees were totally beyond my father's humble means, and the glittering prizes, forever out of his reach.

When arriving here, he enquired as to the cost to join this small, local club, and just because it was small and local, the joining and green fees were within a budget that he decided that he could afford.

What he hadn't taken into account was that in England, as with many other parts of the world, joining a golf or tennis club is to join the elite in that society.

J.J. was certainly not part of the elite of any society, and his application was immediately and unceremoniously rejected.

After his coup-d'état, and his purchase of the local works, suddenly, his application was rediscovered and immediately accepted.

My father's response, which I later realised was an intrinsic part of his character, was to graciously accept their invitation, on the clear understanding that each and every member of the application committee would be barred from the club for life.

To begin with, the club refused this deal, it was only when he suggested that certain members of his workforce; who were members, family of members or good friends of members, might find their jobs becoming redundant for the factory's functioning, that the club ceded to his request.

My father did have a rather tough streak, especially when his pride was put into question.

There was the time that Maman decided that we should have a butler; a perfect gentleman, ramrod straight, beautifully spoken, always impeccably dressed.

Quite the opposite of my father's, all too casual attire, rough language and slouchy, ambling walk.

One Saturday afternoon, my father became unreasonably irritated by the state of the pathway, as he was expecting a guest that he had never met before.

And, due to a lack of availability of anyone else to be instructed to clean it, took a broom and started to brush it himself.

This was not such an unusual occurrence; as he was not above doing any menial task himself, if he decided that it needed doing, and now, and at a moment that there was no-one else around to do it.

This might include vacuuming the stair carpets, at 2 o'clock in the morning, if the dog had the audacity to track its muddy paws through the house, after the staff had left for the night.

Unfortunately, by happenstance, two other events coincided with his cleaning operation; firstly, the butler came out to the terrace to take a break and smoke a cigarette.

At the same moment, a car drove up and a young gentleman get out, my father's guest. He quickly leant the brush against a tree and went up to greet him.

The man glanced, first at my father, then at the butler, elegantly leaning on a post, smoking his cigarette, and asked, in the politest of manners,

'Please inform Mr. Ferguson that Mr. Foster has arrived'.

'Please inform Mr. Foster that Mr. Ferguson would like him off his property in the next 30 seconds and please to never contact him EVER again!'

The poor bemused man first looked to the butler, who quickly finished his cigarette, and returned into the house, and then at my father.

It only took a few more seconds for the penny to drop.

'Oh, Mr. Ferguson, I am so terribly sorry, I do so hope that you can forgive me for my silly mistake.'

'Mr. Foster, you have ten seconds left before I call the police,' and with that, he turned and walked back into the house.

Mr. Foster we never saw nor heard of again, and the butler was packed and out before the end of the afternoon.

This was a story, repeated, from time to time, often at the dinner table, by my father himself, he seemed to take a certain pleasure in revealing just how reactive and unreasonable, he was capable of being.

At what moments, one might inquire, would my parents, who seemed painfully absent during my early years, be sharing their dining table with me?

9.   Dinner is served

In fact, from the age of seven years, I was to eat, twice a month, the Friday evening meal with my two parents, although, it quickly became more often alone with Maman, as J.J. was often 'detained' elsewhere.

The reason for this in-habitual proximity with my mother was due to an event that happend; during a birthday party which I was invited to, by some girl because she was the daughter of one of Maman's friends'.

My mother glanced over at the 'child's table', during the luncheon, and was, 'totally humiliated', (her own words of course), by my total lack of 'any' table manners. So she decided to take things immediately into hand, and installed the bi-monthly, family, evening meal.

I was supposed to be incredibly appreciative of the generosity of my parents to offer to accept my eating with them.

In reality, it was the most awful torture for me, even after Jean-Jacques became old enough to participate in our educative evenings.

Maman had been taught table etiquette as a natural acquisition during her young childhood, as she, and her sister regularly ate with their parents, since they were very young.

To arrive at seven years old, without ever having to worry about how one conveyed one's food from the bowl or plate, into the mouth.

Just as long as it arrived at its destination without losing a part of the cargo onto; the table, one's clothes or one's face, only to be confronted with the complexities of correct social dining behaviour was quite a shock, to say the least.

Not only was I to learn; how to sit, where to place my arms, (they should rest on the edge of the table, with two thirds of the forearm visible), which knives, forks and spoons, one was supposed to use.

How to hold the service, to cut up the food, to place it into one's mouth, how much and how long to masticate it and the correct fashion to swallow the perfectly chopped and churned product.

 All the while, participating in polite and interesting general conversation.

The shock of hearing my mother ask me; as to what I had been doing over the last weeks, how my school career was progressing and how my social life was developing, was enough to get me to question if she had not been abducted by aliens and replaced by an android or a programmed clone.

It was only when I quickly realised that she had absolutely no interest what-so-ever in my responses, that I was comforted, that it was really her.

My father, when he succeeded to arrive before the end of the meal, (that is when he arrived at all), softened greatly the experience, even if he was often already fairly drunk. It was during these shared meals, that I gleaned the scraps of their histories, histories that I have or will share in this document.

I found out many years later, that those family evening meals, were, increasingly over the years, often the only times of the month, that he succeeded to arrive early enough to eat with my mother.

'Well, hello laddie, what a pleasure to see you joining us for supper,' he would then tangent off into some, long rambling story of dubious authenticity.

Maman, who admittedly had a slightly beak shaped nose and closely placed, dark piercing eyes, seemed to metamorphose into some sort of eagle creature. No matter where she appeared to be looking, throughout the whole meal, she really never took her beady eyes off of me.

'Pierre-Alain, asseyez vous correctement, s'il vous plait.' (It was only many years later that I became aware, just how weird it was that Maman 'vous-vouyered' us, being the verbs' conjugation used to show respect, social distance or for referring to several persons at once).

It was also difficult for J.J., who, also lacking the correct social education, was not that much better mannered than I was. He often had to keep himself in check, to not contradict my mother's instructions, as he was demonstrating beautifully, exactly what she was criticising me for doing.

It was during one of these family dinners that a very weird event occurred; I actually had a conversation with my mother, and, miracle of miracles, we happened to agree on something.

'Pierre-Alain, je trouve que vous êtes arrivé à l'âge d'apprendre de monter un cheval'.

'Say, what ?', J.J. had just entered into the room, and although, through the years, he had accepted to study French, he had to really concentrate to follow what was being said.

'Pierre-Alain, is more that old enough to start horse riding lessons, in fact, I will also inscribe Jean-Jacques for some courses of initiation.'

'Real horses?'

Bien sûr, de vrais chevaux'.

'Comme un chevalier ?'

'Nous avons sûrement eu des chevaliers dans notre famille. C'est dans votre sang.'

'What's in his blood? Should we send him to the doctor?'

'J.J. please try to follow the conversation', she turned, slightly irritated, 'I was saying that riding is in his blood, we surely had noble knights, in our past'.

'I can remember some noble nights in my own past', he mumbled and gave me a sly wink.

Maman's look of total disapproval made it more than clear that I was to disregard this remark and to forget to have ever heard it.

After a year or so of this arrangement, Jean-Jacques, although not yet six years old, was also included in these educational evenings.

Jean-Jacques, apart from being the 'Benjamin' and therefore being, from my point of view, a little spoiled by my parents, (they seemed less demanding of him), had the huge advantage that I had two years to learn how to get things right for our parents, he just had to slip in behind my wake, and copy me.

And so it was for the meals; from the first moment, he totally ignored our parents, fixing his big brown eyes on me, he faithfully copied every move, every gesture, every cut, every chew, every swallow.

Maman was incredibly pleased, 'comme vous êtes sage; très bien, quelle politesse'.

I didn't hate Jay, as I called him, not until later, in fact, at that time, even though I was a little jealous of him, we were best of friends.

To tell the truth, if we hadn't shared a room, until I was quite old, I don't know how I would have survived.

10.   My Worst Nightmare

You see, from a very early age, I was plagued with nightmares.

There were several themes that repeated with slight variations; there was that of my parents leaving to go somewhere, somewhere good. They would take Jay out with them, but I always had to do or finish something, or I couldn't find something, so they left first.

Then I would panic that they would leave without me and I would run out after them, to catch them up. The house, being a mansion house, had two stone lions on either side of the front door, it was because of these awful adversaries that I never caught up with the others.

The lions would shoot nets at me, zap me with electric shocks, trip me up, jump on me or even once, create an impenetrable force field.

Even if I succeeded eventually to pass, it was always too late, the others we gone and I was left alone.

A second nightmare was being followed by someone or something; I would run into the kitchen and hide under the kitchen table and force myself to 'go to sleep', that way the being couldn't get to me.

The last nightmare, no big surprises here, was the family dinner; I would be trying to eat correctly, but something would always go wrong, a glass or cup would spill liquid every time I'd try to drink something, or I would forget how to speak French, or the knives and forks would multiply and turn into impossible shapes, so that they were hopeless to try to eat with.

Always, always, Jay would be perfect, Maman would smile at him and sigh when she noticed my inability to behave correctly.

For years, I'd simply get up and go into Marie-Madeleine's room and get into her bed and go back to sleep.

I don't know at what moment Maman became aware of this arrangement, but she insisted that it stop 'immediately'.

So instead I tried to go into her room, but it was locked from the inside, I tried knocking, but to no avail, so I just curled up and waited, and waited, but she didn't come out.

Suddenly, (I must have fallen asleep, just the same), there was J.J., teetering over me.

'What you doin' here laddie?'

'I had a nightmare, I was scared.'

'You'll no get in there, come, you can sleep with me.'

I was shocked and surprised by the offer, but I accepted just the same. It was clear that he was really quite drunk, the scotch on his breath was overwhelming and he stunk of old sweat and cigars.

'You're always welcome wi' me', he threw off his clothes and fell onto the bed, already snoring. I thought about joining him, his bed was easily big enough, but he just revolted me, so I left.

The nightmare now seemed so long and far away that all I could feel was the cold and a great tiredness, so I quietly went back to my own bed and fell asleep.

The next time I had a nightmare, I didn't know what to do, so I sat down and called out for Marie-Madeleine, I didn't have to call for long.

Like a mother hears her baby crying, even from a distance, Marie-Madeleine heard me, and she came to look after me. She tucked me back into my bed, stroked my hair and sang to me,

'Fais dodo, Colas mon p'tit frère', until I fell back asleep.

This only happened a few times before my mother found out about this too and decided on drastic action; after we were both in bed, she locked our door, so that I couldn't call Marie-Madeleine to me.

'Vous êtes un grand garçon, maintenant, vous n'en avez plus besoin.'

I wake up in the night, not because of a nightmare but because I needed to go to the toilet.

Maman hadn't thought of that contingency and by the time I had succeeded to get someone to open the door, I had wet myself.

I don't know if my mother's reaction was reasonable or somehow, the sight of my standing there in a pool of my own urine, made her feel so guilty that her only way to cope was to do something extreme, but she somehow turned the fault onto Marie-Madeleine and insisted that she move out of house immediately.

It was from that time onwards that I took refuge in Jay's bed when the night horrors appeared. I feel sure that he must have noticed, but he never, ever once mentioned it.

11.   Be a Man, My Son

She was found a small, pretty house in the village, which I visited often, as even on her, 'days off', she had nothing better to do than look after us.

This was the first of the major changes that was to punctuate my growing up; the second was leaving the kindergarten, junior school building, to start senior school elsewhere in town.

I had never had to learn to, 'look after myself', all the kids that I mixed with, I'd known since I was little more than a baby.

In the new school there were big kids that I didn't know, boys from quite rough backgrounds, who didn't think twice about stopping a smallish, shy dark haired boy with an unusual beakish nose and deep-set brown eyes.

'Do you 'ave any sweets or pocket money?'

'Why do you want to know?'

'Because I'm going to look after you, and I want to be paid for it.'

'What happens if I don't want to be looked after by you?'

'This..,' and he roughly pushed me over. I was not at all expecting that and fell down quite heavily, I hurt my hand and ripped a bit of the elbow of my new jacket. I gave the boy all that I had on me.

'Every Monday, or else'. I ran into my new school, my very first day, only just succeeding not to cry.

'Qu'est ce que vous avez fait?' Maman screamed at me as I came home on seeing the state of the new jacket.

She didn't stop complaining about how bad I was; to me, to Jay and finally to J.J. when he returned home.

'Come here son, tell me what happened.'

I wasn't sure how much to tell him, you see, I didn't know him that well. Maman, her reactions were easy to predict, but my father, I didn't know.

As usual, he had already starting drinking before arriving home, I looked closely at him, trying to judge what was best to say.

'Looks like you fell over.'

'Yes, sir.'

'Somebody help you?'

'Pardon?'

'Somebody help you to fall over?'

'Yes', I mumbled.

'Y'are quite small and weak, not much good in a tumble, but y'are my son, which means that you're smart. Listen, everyone's got a weakness and everyone's got strengths.

You need to find out what are your strengths and what are his weaknesses', then go in strong, you don't always get a second chance. Now get yee to bed.'

I was both relieved and disappointed; relieved that I wasn't further rebuked, but disappointed that knowing that I was being bullied, he didn't think to do more to help me.

I tossed and turned in my bed, 'it was alright for him, he was never in a position where people didn't do what he wanted, he never had to fight, … or had he?'

I started to think about some of the stories that I had heard over the dinner table, J.J. was a bit like briar rabbit, he always found a way to twist himself out of anything.

I could also be tricky, someone once said that you could move the earth of you found a lever big enough, so what lever would I need to control my new found adversary?

Monday morning came and he was waiting for me at the school gate.

'What do have for me?'

'Your name's Brian Waterfield.'

'What of it?'

'My name's Pierre-Alain Ferguson.'

'So?'

'Your father works at the New Chapel Engineering works.'

'What of it?'

'My father owns 'New Chapel Engineering.'

'So?'

'Are you really that stupid?'

'Your father wouldn't sack my father.'

'Why don't you go and ask him if my father's capable of sacking someone because he didn't like something that they had done, even outside of work.' I didn't offer to give him anything, and he didn't ask.

The next Monday, I got to school early, I was waiting at the gate for him.

'What have you got in your pockets?'

'What's it to you?'

'The shoe is now on the other foot, give me.'

And so he did. I could have shook down every kid in the school, and, from time to time, I did benefit from a subtly, veiled threat, but I was 'sage', I didn't need to abuse that edge too often.

Of course, by the time that Jay started school, everyone knew in advance, who he was, (I'd seen to that), so his school life was pretty much smooth sailing from day one.

12. Life's Swings and Roundabouts

'Where is Marie-Madeleine?'

'Elle ne travaille plus chez nous.'

'What ? Since when ?'

'Vous êtes grands, vous n'avez plus besoin d'elle. C'est reglé.'

I waited until J.J. returned that evening.

'Is it true that Marie-Madeleine has been sacked?'

'Aye lad, she's gone.'

'Just like that, like an old sock? After all that she's done for us?'

'Your mother has decided that she is no longer useful, so she was given notice. After all, she was only an employee.'

'No, she wasn't, she was family, she IS family.'

'I'm sorry Jamie, (he rarely called me by my middle name), but it was your mother's decision, I just deal with the formalities.'

'But what will she do?'

'Oh I wouldn't worry too much on her behalf, she's a fine head on her shoulders. I've been thinking for some time that the factory would do well to have its own nursery and your mother has some friends that are looking to take some classes in French, both for themselves and for their children. Marie-Madeleine is not likely to starve.'

 I was not at all placated; full of anger and righteous indignation, despite the lateness of the hour, I threw on my coat and ran over to her little house.

I did knock before rushing in, but only just.

'Why hello Pierre-Alain, qu'est ce qui c'est passé?'

'I just found out that you have been …', I didn't get to finish my sentence, for I had just noticed that she wasn't alone.

'Oh, please let me introduce my new neighbour, Muriel Miller and this is her daughter, Angelique. And this crazy, young man, is the closest thing that I have to a son, Pierre-Alain James Ferguson.'

(This was the first time that I'd ever heard her speak English, but that wasn't to be the greatest shock of the evening).

I stiffly shook the hand of the lady, 'a pleasure.' I then turned to the young woman, true to her name, here, facing me was an honest to God angel.

'Hi', it was all that I could manage, I turned and ran out of the house as fast as I could, I felt like I was going to be sick.

The Island of Survival

13. Landing

The fog starts to lift, he finds himself on a barren rock; behind, the sea is violently attacking the shoreline, smacking it savagely with a blind rage, as if its very presence was somehow an affront to its right to dominate the earth.

In front, there is a rough plane, with patches of vegetation, which are somewhere wrong, but he cannot make out exactly why, for the moment. Further inland, he can see an enormous forest, a forest the like he had never seen or maybe heard of, the trees are huge, yes a few majestic redwoods maybe, but this was a whole forest of them, as far as the eyes could see.

The wind tests to see if he is capable of flight, it almost succeeds to lift him off the ground, but it is still not quite strong enough, so it gives that up, and frustrated, pushes him heavily to the hard rocky floor.

So, here he lays, angry and hurt, he rolls over onto his back, he looks up and a little back.

'What the?'

'Something wrong?'

'Everything is wrong, but the sky and the sun…'

'Ah'.

'Why is the sun red and the sky turquoise?'

'Why is anything the way it is? I believe that it has something to do with the composition of the atmosphere.'

A shadow softly crosses over his face, from behind, cutting off the sun.

'What the …?' He turns and sits up, the figure is short, heavy set, somewhere a cross between a man and a small gorilla, wearing some sort of animal skin, to protect his privates. 'Is that you?'

'To ask if I am, who I am, is a question that warrants not a response.'

'But what are you?'

'The same as you.'

'You must be joking, you look like some kind of missing link.'

'Why not take a moment to look at your own hands?'

'My hands? Oh-my-God, these are not my hands.' They are short, wide, heavy, strong and very hairy, the finger nails black and claw like.

'They are now.'

'What have you done to me?'

'You are on the island of survival, here you will learn … how to survive.'

'But, I know how to survive.'

'What do you know?'

'I need to make a hut, start a fire.'

'Start a fire, quite right, and how do you start a fire?'

'I, I, I don't remember. How can I not remember how to make a fire?'

'Remind me, what's a wheel?'

'Stupid question, a wheel is a … it's a … a … thing.'

'What does it do?'

'I can't remember, I can't remember. What the Hell have you done to me?'

'This is a representation of a period of history, sort of like the stone age.'

'I know what the stone-age is. How can I remember that, but not what a wheel is.'

'This is like a sort of a dream; sometimes we know things that we didn't know, sometimes we can't even remember our own names.'

'What's the point of all this?'

'As I have said, you are to relearn to survive.'

'Like this?'

'Like that.'

'So, what do I need to do so that I can get out of here?'

'Hunt, kill, protect yourself.'

'And if I don't?'

'Then you will get hungry, cold, wet and maybe hurt.'

'But I cannot die, I can't get hungry or hurt.'

'Can you feel hunger and pain, in a dream?'

'So if I don't do the things that you want, then I will suffer?'

'I don't care what you do or don't do, but if you don't do the things that are necessary for survival, yes, you will suffer.'

'Will you help me?'

'I am only here to help.'

'Great, let's get started then.'

'I am sorry, we seem to have a slight misunderstanding, I am here to help you, in, how should I put it, in a sort of advisory capacity, for the practical stuff, sorry, you're rather on your own.'

'And exactly what would you advise me to be doing, in your advisory capacity, if I might dare to ask?'

'Of course, well, as the sun tends to heat up these rocks, rather a lot by the afternoon, maybe it would be, not such a bad idea, to go a seek out some shade.'

He gets up, turning to the forest, 'how far do you think it is to the forest?'

There is no answer, he turns back towards the man, but he is no longer there.

'Great', and with that, the short, stubby man creature, starts to make his lumbering way to the protection of the forest.

'I say one thing for this thing of a body, Jimmy boy, it's bloody fit. Jimmy boy? How long since I've thought of myself as Jimmy boy? How long since I've been talking t' me-self?

Okay, just this stretch of red sand, it is bloody red, isn't it? Bloody red, like that, quite clever really. Starting to get hot, my feet hurt, I should do something about that.

I'm sure I know something so that me feet don't hurt on the hot ground, maybe I'll remember later. Just keep going, nearly there, nearly there, okay, that's better, good forest, cool on the feet.'

'What the hell am I doing? What warped, sick game is he playing at? Anyway, who is he? Maybe it's just a creation of my own unconscious, that's what it must be.

I'm dying or dead, and I've created some sort of fantasy reality, so as to deal with the guilt of committing suicide.

Well, I'm not going to play anymore. I didn't want to live anymore, and I've no interest in some sort of experience of atonement.

Listen God, if this is your idea, sorry but I'm not interested, if I'm to go to Hell, well it's no more than I deserve, just stop this charade and let's get on with it.'

He waits for a response, a reaction, but nothing happens.

'Well, I'm going to make myself comfortable in this tree, and when you get bored, then you can do what you want.'

He does as he promises, climbs a tree and settles himself to wait.

14. Tribal Matters

Some time later he stirs himself.

'Shit, even if I'm dead, I need to pee.'

He descends the tree and relieves himself.

'What's that?! What's there? Oh-my-God!'

The creatures resembles a huge bear.

'It surely can't hurt me, I'm not really here.'

He stands facing the great beast, undecided whether to climb back up the tree, run or trust in his logic of being un-damageable.

The beast advances, surprisingly quickly for such a massive creature. His indecision has given the bear the moment that it needed, before he can move, it swings its right paw and he is propelled from the ground.

He lands heavily, several feet away, it has struck him on the upper right arm, which is already painful and bleeding.

The blow has also winded and disorientated him, and he lays on the soft ground, watching it advance towards him, unable to react other than curl up into a ball, and experience the rising panic, of being in an impossible situation with no possible means of escape.

Suddenly, there are loud screams, and a shower of stones land on the bears' enormous furry body. It turns, screams back in anger and in pain, searching for the source of this outrage.

Again more screams from the trees, another rain of missiles and the bear turns and runs off, whether to attack the stone throwers or to escape them, he cannot guess. That the bear has left, that is the only information of any interest.

Some moments pass before anything else happens.

Then, from somewhere out of the trees, a figure emerges, it resembles the form of the other man, but it is not him.

'Duncan, it's you, what are you doing here?'

The short, squat humanoid continues towards him; he looks at the fallen man and grunts.

'How can you be Duncan? You don't look like Duncan, but I know that you are him, weird.'

The other man still continues to advance cautiously towards him, the similarity to a gorilla is troubling. He hesitates before coming close enough to contact, then, very slowly, he reaches out his stubby hand to take the injured arm and examine it. He moves it gently, he is testing whether it is broken or not.

'Aw,' Faron cries out in pain, and flinches. The other man, whom Faron calls Duncan, immediately drops the arm and jumps back in alarm, he crouches down in a defensive posture.

'Sorry, didn't mean to startle you, here', he offers him his arm, so that Duncan can continue with the examination, but the other stays in his crouch, then starts to rock gently, forwards and backwards.

Not knowing what he is supposed to do, Faron, forces himself into a similar position, tries to look friendly and mimics the rocking movement.

The two men continue this for some moments, other men and some women, came into view, crouch down, some feet away and join in, in the rocking.

He is intrigued to notice that the women look, to him, very similar to those of the men, their faces, although hairless, have the same heavy look, they have almost the same shape, none of the usual thinner waist and wider hips, only a little smaller.

And; as for the breasts themselves, which are, not at all covered, they are more like men's chests than that of the women of his experience, only slightly bigger, rounder, and, as opposed to all the men, not hairy.

Duncan grunts, the swaying stops and he gets up. Faron and others follow his lead, and then they turn and head back through the forest. Other than a few grunts, there is no sound from any of them, they just follow Duncan, in single file, back to the camp.

The camp is relatively large; there are a number of round wooden huts, although there are still people living in the caves behind the village

There are some types of species of sheep and of pigs penned up, as well as a large number of very wolf-like dogs hanging around.

Further out, Faron can see that they have also begun to invest in agriculture, a field of wheat can be seen as he enters the village.

Duncan grunts and points towards Faron, clearly they have some sort of rudimentary language, but it is much too foreign for the modern man to interpret.

A young women comes towards him, she is small and shy, it is Angelique. Faron is confused, he has loved and hated, given and stolen from her, but this prehistoric Angelique, knows nothing of all that, she is just a part of this construction, based on people from his past.

She stops in front of him, too shy and too scared to advance further, Duncan notices this and shouts a rough order to her.

She reacts with a passing moment of fear, but that quickly subsides, she is now more frightened of his anger than of this unknown stranger.

So she goes up to Faron, gently takes him by his good arm and leads him off.

She, like all the others, is short, squat, heavy and in hardly any aspects, what he would call feminine.

Never, would he imagine to label her as beautiful, and yet, she is her.

The softness, gentleness and caring continues, she takes him to a cleared space outside one of the huts, sits him down, cleans his wound and covers it with a paste made from some type of moss and clay.

Faron is drown back to his memories of the early days with Angelique, when they were young, innocent, free and effortlessly falling in love. This Angelique is young, innocent and free of all their sordid future history.

She knows nothing of his upcoming deceits and betrayals; of his anger and violence towards her, of his disappointments and deceptions of her un-understandable attitudes and behaviours.

No, this Angelique is a reset model, 'table rase', a fresh start, and she was his first love, maybe his only love, and here she is; as pure and as beautiful as the first day that they met in Marie-Madeleine's little house.

No matter that there is no physical resemblance between the two, they are one and the same, and he has no choice, it is happening again, he is falling in love with Angelique.

Life with the savages, as he thinks to call them, is physically tough, but there is enough to eat, although meat is rare, the shelters are sufficient, they protect quite well from both the sun and the rain, and general daily life is quite acceptable, after one gets used to the washing and toiletry conditions.

The almost constant feeling of danger takes some getting used to; everyone can seem to be quite comfortable and relaxed, but it only takes a certain movement in the closer trees for everyone to react and for some of the men to jump up and take up their weapons.

In fact, Faron, is surviving quite well, the only problem is Angelique. Angelique is Duncan's mate, although he can feel that she is also attracted to him, she is much too scared of the tribes' leader to get close to him.

Before his depression and weight problems, (both, obviously linked), he had always had a particularly active sex life, now, forced out of his depressive state, his sexual appetite had also been revived.

He is feeling frustrated, even though he has succeeded to 'mate' with some of the younger, as yet, non-attached females, it is not at all satisfying, he finds them primitive, rough and he almost has the feeling of participating in some advanced form of bestiality.

'I suppose that I could try to see if he might share, God, it's worth a try.' So he waits until he finds himself alone with Duncan and Angelique.

'So,' he gives a timid smile in Duncan's direction, 'how would it be if we both shared Angelique?'

He walks slowly up to her and gently takes her by the wrist, they seem intrigued by this gesture. He then starts to pull her away, towards the little hut that he has made his own.

She does not resist, and allows herself to be led towards his boudoir, Duncan follows some feet behind.

All seems to go well until he moves to take her into the dwelling, Duncan grunts, it doesn't seem like a good sign.

'It's okay,' he smiles, winningly towards the husband,

'I'm just sharing your mate; be logical, be optimistic, let's create a rota.' Duncan begins to emit a low, growling sound, like an old grinding machine.

Faron stops at the threshold, not so sure of himself; Angelique is showing more and more signs of distress, her breathing has speeded up, her pupils are open and her eyes flicker from man to man, she is tensing up, flight or fight?

Duncan stops moving forward, is that a good sign?

Duncan stops growling, surely a good sign.

Duncan sinks into a half squat, maybe not a good sign.

Duncan turns his hands as if getting ready to grab something, probably not a good sign.

Duncan waits, immobile, this is surely a clear sign of something.

Faron does not choose to continue his experiment.

Faron does not wish to test if this is a good or bad sign.

Faron has been in many a bar fight, often over a woman.

Faron does not know how Duncan fights.

Faron sighs, releases Angelique's arm, waves at Duncan, and enters his space, alone.

Of course the story doesn't end there, Faron is still drawn towards her, still feeling frustrated and, over time, coping less and less well with all that.

For the moment, he is starting to feel better; the healthy environment, the necessity of a certain amount of physical work, being accepted by everyone, without having to explain anything, (not that anyone could understand anything that he said).

He enjoys the clean taste of the fresh food, meat, when available is a treat, (certain members of the tribe have learn the trick of lighting fires using flint and pyrite rocks, one of them reminds him of Jean-Jacques), and joy of all joys, there is even beer to drink.

Whether this is historically correct, or just a positive construction of his unconscious, he doesn't care in the least, it is certainly a great plus in this life experience.

So, yes, it is true, he is starting to enjoy things again, he even acknowledges that he is experiencing a certain amount of pleasure.

And then, there is the hunt.

15.   Will you go hunt, my Lord?

The Duncan, from Faron's past was always a cautious man; this incarnation seems no different.

Although for generations his tribe had survived as hunter-gatherers, he preferred animal husbandry and farming as a lifestyle rather than take the risk of injury and death, which the hunting of large animals implicated.

However, from time to time, a large predator would take it into its tiny mind, that the camp is an interesting source of alimentation. With the larder generously stocked with sheep and pigs, held tantalisingly available, just for the taking.

The members of the tribe would try to drive it off, but if this attempt was unsuccessful, finally, Duncan would accept the inevitable to prepare to hunt it down and kill it.

By happenstance, one such occurrence happened some weeks after Faron had arrived.

Faron is not foolhardy by nature; but over the past years, he had indulged in more and more risky undertakings, in an attempt to break out of downward spiral of doom and despair that was dogging his life like the omnipresent rainstorms in the life of a character in a Douglas Adams' novel.

His is also excited to try out his new invention; it is a way to propel small spears, by using a bent branch, attached on both ends by a length of tough vine.

Although the vine often breaks and has to be replaced, the small spears travel further than one can throw a regular size one.

Duncan and the other members of the tribe have looked on to the creation of this weapon with little interest, and the closest that Faron has seen to the expression of amusement.

He has spent quite a long time working on this, making a handful of the small spears, and learning how to best use them.

The night before the hunt, the tribe undertakes a type of ritual; first, they squat into their sitting positon and rock and chant, (that would be the closest interpretation that Faron could find).

Large quantities of beer are served, while the rocking and chanting continues. Then, one by one, the members start to move, in what one could only describe as a form of dance.

Duncan disappears from the congregation, moving quietly and intently towards one of the older caves, one no longer used as a dwelling. Only to reappear some time later carrying a spear, if one looks closely, one might also notice that the fingers of his right hand are coloured by an orange-brown stain.

This is a signal, from out of the shadows, one of a larger tribesmen, rushes out, growling and shrieking.

The others scatter, screaming as if in great fear. The 'beast' advances; sometimes upright, sometimes on all fours, aiming directly for Duncan. Duncan stops, screams at the beast to leave, and shakes his spear to re-enforce his command.

The beast stops for a moment, as if contemplating its choices, but this is only to take a breath before, screaming with all its force it rushes headlong towards the lone hunter.

The matador takes a swipe at it as it rushes forward, the corrida has begun; the bull-like attacks are fast and furious.

Once, twice, three times it passes; then it makes contact, Duncan is driven back and trips heavily onto the hard earth.

The mad thing turns again, it is time for the kill, it starts to run again, bellowing in its crazy bloodlust, it's going to crush him under its great hooves, closer and closer, time stretches out like a freezing droplet, the people gasp, they tense, their eyes dilate, is this the end of their leader?

He approaches, ever so slowly, at full gallop, he is almost on top of him when, as if out of nowhere, the spear appears, its head pointing exactly towards the oncoming adversary, who, unable to stop, runs directly into it.

In the semi-darkness, they watch as the head and part of the shaft appear to erupt through its back, it stops, just for the shortest of moments, then wavers, and then heavily falls.

There is silence, no-one moves, Duncan gets up, wrenches his spear from the inert beast and thrusts it into the air in a universal gesture of victory.

The crowd erupts, they rush towards him, Faron only just stops himself from chanting, 'we are the champions, we are the champions', the energy is electric, they are ecstatic.

Nobody seems to notice when the dead beast, discreetly rolls over and gets back up onto his feet, before joining the rest of the tribe in a celebratory final beer.

The morning is clear and still quite cold; the drinking of beer at any hour of the day was something that Faron is starting to get used to.

It reminds him of his period of being on alcoholic, when the best protection from getting a hangover, was to stay permanently drunk.

Duncan, although the clear leader of the tribe, is not the head-huntsman, this task was left to a younger man, who Faron feels reminds him of his other best friend, Mike.

Mike was a predator, Mike was a fighter, a killer, Mike wanted, Mike would succeed, Mike was dangerous.

Yes, this one reminded him well enough of his Mike.

Faron notices the fear in the eyes of the women as they watch their men prepare for battle; as it must have been in tens of thousands of mornings just like this one all throughout history.

'Will my partner, father, brother, child, return, whole, safe and sound, or not?'

There is nothing to do, just to look at them, one last time, fixing the image of the loved one, onto the delicate kodachrome of their fragile human memories.

Mike makes a sign to Duncan, Duncan grunts, the tribesmen turn to pick up their weapons, a variety of clubs and spears.

The silent goodbyes of the women, are far more elegant and touching than Faron has ever seen or heard.

Mike starts out, the rest follow, for once Duncan takes the rear. This is not to protect himself, his task is to protect the group from any predator that might attack from behind.

Faron is almost directly behind Mike, but not quite.

He wishes to watch how he functions, but still to keep several people between himself and the head of the group.

After all, he is here to learn about survival, there is no need to get himself mauled to death, (even if he must recover), when a certain amount of good sense might avoid such unpleasantness.

Faron has gotten to the point where he has, to some degree forgotten, just how close to animals the tribe resembles,

Mike seems to revert almost totally to some form of former state. He advances, more often on all fours, smelling and tasting the earth and plants in his path.

Suddenly there is a change in his attitude, the flowing, fluid motion of his movements, ceases, he stops, sniffs, sniffs again, stiffens, straightens his little body and turns back to the group.

Without a sound, he raises an arm high into the air, this is the signal, he has found the trail; a wave of excitement, arousal, fear and expectation sweeps down the ranks.

Then he turns back, and they are again making their way through the foliage.

'I wonder how we shall capture it. Maybe we should hunt it like a Snark.

They sought it with thimbles, they sought it with care;
* They pursued it with forks and hope;*
They threatened its life with a railway-share;
* They charmed it with smiles and soap.'*

He is lost in his thoughts; maybe he is fighting a growing feeling of fear, maybe he has never, in the sober light of day, put himself into a situation where he could be physically damaged.

He allows himself to dissociate from the moment, part totally present, totally aware of every sight, sound and smell, (thanks to his prehistoric senses), yet another, protective filter, loses himself in Lewis Carroll, and the nonsense and the rhymes.

Something is happening; his breathe is shorter and shallower, his heart is beating faster, his muscles are becoming more and more tense, every sound, every shadow, every smell becomes profoundly important.

They are approaching their prey, they will soon be participating in a life or death struggle, they will be involved with a fight for survival, this is not a game, this is for real!

'Okay, Jamie, this is it. No Friday night brawl outside a nightclub, with a few sharp blades, this is a big, dangerous bugger.

So why am not feeling the fear? I should be thinking of running away, this is not my fight, this is only some kind of dream, I don't need to do this, I can just say no.'

They exit the forest, there is a clearing, behind the clearing there is the entrance to a massive cave. This is the lair of the great bear, maybe the exact same beast that he had encountered on his first day on this island.

'So what are they going to do now, I wonder, it would be suicide to rush into there, even with the spears and all?'

They have all left the protection of the trees, Duncan appears the last. They look at him, and he grunts back at them.

Most of the warriors turn to face the cave mouth, spears at the ready, while **Jean-Jacques**, a 'fire-maker', as Faron had entitled him, digs into his animal skin pouch and extracts two stones and a handful of dry moss, some others disappear back into the forest.

Jay bends down quite close to the entrance and busies himself with the delicate art of fire making, he has quite a lot of experience of this and the little fire is soon started.

The men return with armfuls of damp moss, small twigs and branches, the fire smokes and burns.

Mike looks to Duncan, who nods slightly, clearly a natural signal of agreement since the very dawn of time. Mike walks over to the fire, takes a bigger branch and pushes the smoking mass further and further into the cave.

Somewhere, within the mountain, there must be another exit for the air, for the smoke becomes more and more drawn into the emptiness, the space outside is once again clear.

And yet, there is still some smoke in Faron's head, the waiting had left too much space for his idling consciousness.

He is picturing in his mind the reaction of Angelique as he was leaving, which then linked with the hunt in hand, which in turn segues into something else.

'Will you go hunt, my lord?

What, Curio?

The hart. [*The heart - ed*]

Why, so I do, the noblest that I have'.

It is a little gag that has always amused him. His amusement is cut short, the bellowing roar of the angry, frightened bear, cuts immediately through his reverie. The group tenses; rocks and spears at the ready.

'This is fucking dangerous, I must be out of my bleeding mind. I came here to learn about survival, what in God's name is facing a nine foot, fucking, furious bear got to do with learning about survival?

But if I run, what then? If the others get hurt or killed and I've run away, that makes me worse than a coward, I would be also partly responsible, and God only knows, I've enough guilt to deal with as it is.

Anyway, I, at least, can't be killed, and I really would like to prove that my mini spear thingy, can work.'

This quite long reflection, took, in reality, only a few seconds, and he is ready with the rest of them as the enraged creature rushes into the open. The men shout and scream and throw rocks and spears at monstrous animal.

There is a moment of hesitation; it experiences a moment of fear, no, a moment of terror, the pupils shrink to two tiny pinpricks of black, but it too knows about survival, and for this creature, survival means being more violent and aggressive than those who would attack it.

It bellows again and rushes forward towards the group; Faron takes a deep breath and pulls hard on the taut, vine bow string.

He targets the head, but over-shoots, the missile passes uselessly, a foot above its head. It is still advancing, it seems to be directing itself directly towards him, maybe it remembers him from the experience of his first day on the island, maybe it still has a score to settle against him.

The others are still throwing stones and their spears, but it seems to have little effect on this hairy locomotive train. It is now clearly on track for Faron, and they both know it.

Time, again slows down.

He watches the great bear advancing towards himself.

'I could move, I could run, but I could also just stand here and shoot another little spear.'

He is moving within a dream; the roaring sound has faded, it is continuing to advance, to grow, to fill his whole field of vision. In his slow motion dance, he reaches for another arrow, cocks it into the bow, draws and releases.

The arrow speeds out from the bow and buries itself, deeply into the left side the bear's torso. It howls in rage and pain; Faron is a bad creature, worse than the other bad creatures, his magic is even more bad than theirs, knock it down, knock it dead!

It covers the last few feet in seconds; one simple swipe of its enormous paw and he is again driven to the ground.

t comes forward for a second blow, a fatal blow, but Mike and Duncan are not hunting for the first time.

They expected the bear to break through the first line of men, this was already planned, for now, out of the trees, comes another group, screaming at the top of their lungs, more rocks and more spears.

The bear hesitates for a second time; the momentum of the men, like the angry seas, smashing on the rocky shore, are enough to force the bear to turn and to head back, towards its cave.

But no, the first group have regrouped, more rocks and reclaimed spears shower the bear.

 It screams in anger and in fear; it throws itself at the first group, as if to crush them all, then it can return to its lair, the memory of the fire and smoke, already far from its mind, only the hope of that safe, dark pit, in which it has always been safe.

Diving on the men might have been a reasonable strategy, if not for the second group, following close behind, they jump savagely onto its back, thrusting their spears into its now undefended body, dragging them out, only to plant them even deeper and deeper into the shaking beasts', bloody innards.

It tries to turn, to throw them off, to get back up, to find its safety, to survive, but it is much, much too late.

The beast has weakened, it can only succeed to turn over, lashing out with its great claw, it throws one of the men, off of its back, smashing him into the side of the hill. It then tries to regain its feet, but this time it's Faron,

Faron with his mini spear thingy, he cannot miss, he does not miss, the short spear hurtles towards the bear, catching it straight in the throat.

It gags, it makes as if to try and catch it to pull it out, but the object is much too small for its grasp, and it only has seconds left before its final breath leaves its heavy body, and all is momentarily still and peaceful.

There are injuries, damaged arms and legs and one man with crushed bones on his chest, he might not make it back to the village.

Jean-Jacques runs back to get the women so as to help the injured and to help strip and chop up the bear – this is a job for everyone.

No one gives Faron much attention, which peeves him a little, as he feels that his invention helped secure the victory.

16.   To the Victor belongs the spoils

However, he is on a high after the danger, the brush with death, and the knowledge of the efficiency and power of his thingy.

The after hunt feast is a high point in the life of the tribe; meat to eat, beer to drink, singing and dancing, there are flutes, resonating, wood sticks and smooth, tapping stones.

Duncan, as head of the tribe, cuts the innards of the kill, (the rest has already been cut, cleaned, is cooking or cured); he offers the heart to Mike, as the leader of the hunt, he would be in his right to take it for himself.

'Always the team player, Duncan, always the team player.'

He then pulls out the liver, Faron is interested to see what he will do with this delicacy. To his great surprise, Duncan walks up to him and offers him this token of high esteem. Faron, slightly taken aback, gratefully accepts it.

Duncan grunts, and pantomimes Faron using his primitive bow and arrow, the tribe make a sound, that the new hero translates as a cheer, smiling, he waves back to his public.

He then notices Angelique, quietly standing outside of the light cast by the blazing fire. She is looking at him, straight at him, their eyes meet, and for the shortest of moments, they lose themselves in each other.

Then she starts, a yoyo on a cord, she is spun back, back into her body, the two souls ripped apart.

What was need and desire is savagely replaced by a look of shock and of fear, she knows how dangerous it would be for her to experience those feelings for him.

He has no such restrictions, her reaction only proves and re-enforces his feeling that she is as attracted to him, as he is to her.

'Survival; that is what I am here to learn about; well, that must mean survival of the fittest, and the fastest, and the foxiest. Beauty and the best, that will be our story, that is how it will be.'

The feast continues, everyone, or so it seems, eats, drinks, sings and dances to a state of exhaustion. Faron has eaten and drunk just enough to fire his resolve, Angelique has neither eaten nor drunk anything.

As the fire fades into a flaming memory, one by one the tribes' people return to their caves or huts or just allow themselves to drop onto the beaten earth, softened by layers of food and drink.

Faron hunts out a leather pouch and fills it with food, he them takes up the bow and arrows and turns, only to find Angelique's eyes, staring out from the shadow between two huts.

'Come', she does not move, not towards him, but not away either. He walks, quietly, surely, determinedly towards her. She continues to look directly at him, but remains as inanimate as Pygmalion's statue.

He reaches out to touch her and the fire of the Gods, burning in his wild eyes, flows down and into her stiff body. She shudders, shocked into movement and life, her first reaction is to recoil.

He is holding onto her arm, he absorbs her reaction, allowing his arm to extend away, only for it to gently spring back towards himself and the open space behind him. The yoyo returns to the holder of the string.

This time it is for her to accept the movement; her arm advances towards him, and then, her whole body follows the action, she starts to walk with him, her hand slips silently into his.

Although he is looking forward, directing them out of the camp; he can feel the excitement in the tension of her grip, her breathing is quick and short.

She must be as excited and as scared as he is, but they are escaping to freedom, this is what survival is all about.

He leads, drags her out from the compound, their two hearts beating wild rhythms of danger and adventure.

Picking a path at random, they head out into the wilds of the island.

They trek for some hours until the effects of the danger and excitement become replaced by an increasingly heavy dose of reality, in the forms of tiredness and physical exhaustion.

There is a glade; the sun has just risen enough to warm the air and fill the space with a gently wavering, speckled illumination.

They pile together a mass of fallen leaves, and melt down into it, their two, furry bodies, entwined in complementary shades of light and darker browns.

It must have been some time in the afternoon that they began to regain consciousness.

It had been quite some years since Faron had, had his body wake him to the 'morning erection', an unusual phenomenon, in that it needs no obvious stimulation, neither real nor any fantasy contact with a sexual partner.

Here and now, he is with Angelique, the stimulation is obvious, they are 'spooned', she has her back to him, he is holding her around the waist and breasts.

His erection is strong and present; he presses her tighter into him. She is awake, her body stiffens in excitement, her breathing is stronger, deeper, it almost resembles an animal panting.

She starts to rub herself against him, against his manhood, he increases his pressure; they must release their individuality, they will become one.

He starts to kiss her, but, beyond his conscious will, the kissing becomes biting, they are wreathing, twisting, fighting, emotion takes control, only to give over to the very, very most basic, animal instincts.

He is on top of her; he pins her arms horizontally, but there is no public to see this martyr give her life to his.

He tries to enter her, but to this she resists, twisting her body, first to the left, then to the right. He does not understand, 'what is wrong?', 'why should she resist?'

There is nothing else for it, either he totally compels her with all of his force and frustration, or he gives up and tries to understand the problem.

It is this moment's lack of concentration that gives the opportunity that she needs, like a furry snake, she suddenly twists body, arms and legs, slips out from under him, she is free.

'What will she do? Will she run away, back to Duncan and the camp? Will she just run away? Or will she just wait and try to make him understand what it is that is wrong?'

The outcome was ... none of the above.

She stands up, turns away from him, bends slightly forward, at the same time lifting up her flimsy rag of animal skin.

Faron has had quite an extensive sex life, so this is not something that he has never experienced before. As soon as the message is understood, he is onto his feet, and rushing towards her.

She is quite ready for him; as wet as any woman that he has ever experienced, he slides in, as smooth as any victim is sucked down into a patch of quicksand.

And that is how is seems; his movement and hers, in one simple, smooth, flowing motion, from behind her, to the first contact, to the point of entering, to the moment that she had the whole of his shaft, totally within her wreathing body.

His arms, wrapped around her waist, he pulls, tight, tighter, tighter, digging himself even further inside her, then release, a moment, his penis retracts, the merest of distances.

No long, slow deep, thoughtful sexually here; it is fast, very, very, fast, a roll on the drum fast, a woodpecker pecking fast, a high speed, piston rod fast.

There is no thought, no idea, no time, no space, there is only the movement, and the vibration. But it is everywhere, his body is totally taken; he shakes, he vibrates, he tingles, he sweats.

The world is shifting, spinning, swirling, spiralling, and he is part of all that.

This is being alive, this is survival at its most raw, most rare, most real.

He screams, she screams, the world screams; he must be ejaculating, but it has nothing to do with any experience that he has ever had before.

The world explodes in a million particles of life itself; he is one with every one of the millions of sperm, launched from his own super charged rocket.

And then … it is over.

Again they crumple onto their comforting cot of dried leaves, again intertwined, again exhausted, again ready to release into the depths of unconsciousness, into sleep.

But this time, somewhere, the two individual, independent beings, have become one.

They pass the time collecting fruit and nuts, sleeping and copulating; they succeed to avoid the myriad dangers of the island, and have recreated a sort of Garden of Eden, in which the snake is only welcome as a source of extra protein.

17.   A Sense of Responsibility

In all this time, Faron has had no contact with the entity or person that brought him to the island, fortunately, this is about to change.

Faron is swimming just off the coast, Angelique has already gone back into the forest, to collect some fruit for lunch.

He is beginning to be able to understand some of the basic concepts in her language and communication has become possible.

'You know, that it can get quite hot around lunch time', he mused out loud.

It seemed an eternity since Faron had heard someone speaking in a language that he understood. He stops swimming and looks up towards the shore line.

'So, you're back?'

'What makes you think that I've been away?'

'Well I haven't seen you.'

'When was the last time that you looked at the back of your heel?'

'D'no, maybe months.'

'Does that mean that you haven't had a heel, in all that time?'

'Don't be stupid.'

'However, by the same rule, just because you haven't seen me, doesn't mean that I haven't been here.'

'So why are you here now?'

'Because you need me.'

'I think that I'm doing very well, I have found back my will to live and I'm doing great at surviving.'

'As you have said, until now.'

'What do you mean, until now?'

'It is getting towards midday, which now, I've said three times, that it gets very hot at midday.

"The proof is complete, if only I've stated it thrice."

There is a reference here to something that he surely knows, he also knows that it will trouble him until he can remember where from.

'You are not worried about the heat, then?'

'What? Oh yes, the heat, okay, I'm getting out now.'

He drags himself out of the water and dries off on the damp rocks. It is only when he takes a step towards the trees that he realizes just how hot the ground has become.

'Ouch!' It's bloody hot.' The blood red rocks and sand, where indeed burning hot. 'What am I supposed to do now?'

'What do you want to do?'

'I want to get back to the forest, where it's cool, back to Angelique.'

'Then off you go then.'

'But it's bloody hot.'

'It's only about fifteen feet.' It is true, the distance back to the woods was only about five meters, but those five meters, over burning rocks and sand, could have been five miles, for all Faron cares, it is just impossible to cross.

'It's too hot for me to cross, I'll burn my feet.'

'Actually, no, you can cross that distance, if you walk at a steady pace.'

'Oh no, if I'm to cross that, I'll just have to run for it.'

'No, you will not.'

'Look, first of all you come to warn me of the heat of the sun, after it's too late to do anything about it, now you want me to walk over the red-hot, burning sands, I really don't understand you at all.'

'Then by all means, I will explain. You are here to learn about survival. Please let me finish before you think to interrupt, yes, you have learnt many things about survival so far.

However, one major lesson of survival is the ability to withstand a certain amount of pain.'

'And so you think that I should torture myself and burn my feet, so as to learn this lesson?'

'Not exactly; you see, as I have already stated once, now this makes twice, you are quite capable, everyone is, to walk that distance, even over hot coals, without burning yourself, as long as you walk steadily and regularly, without stopping or slowing down.'

'And what exactly is the trick to that?'

'The trick that I am about to teach you now.'

Faron sits back down on the wave cooled rocks, 'teach away.'

'First and foremost, you must believe fully that you can walk across the heated surface without burning your feet.'

'Maybe it would just be easier if I believed that I was a bird that could fly over the burning sands, and then you could do some of your magic stuff, and pow, it would be true.'

'So you agree that this is an unreal world?'

'Sure'.

'Then it should be easy to believe that you cannot get hurt. Every world, somewhere, is just an illusion.'

'Maybe so, but I can still get hurt and feel pain, that I have already proven.'

'Of course, but what would be the sense of getting you to burn your feet?'

'There was once a Jewish businessman that decided to teach his six year old son about business.'

'I am not following you.'

'This was one of father's favorite stories. So he lifts his son on top of a big chest of draws. Now jump into my arms, directs the father. But I'm scared replies the child.

Don't worry, I'll catch you, responds the father, stretching his arms out to his offspring. Finally, the boy jumps off the furniture, the father lifts up his arms towards his son, then drops them down to his side, the boy lands heavily on the floor. Why did you do that?, he cries from the floor. Now you know, the father replies, in life, don't trust no-one.'

'So you think that I would let you burn yourself so as to teach you a lesson?'

'Why not?'

'Because, young man, this is only the first of seven islands, if I did something to lose your trust now, how can I get you to follow my instructions for the rest?'

'So I should trust you?'

'Trust is the most important factor.'

Faron stops for a moment, shrugs his shoulders and comments, 'anyway, I've got to get back, or else wait here until the sun goes down and the ground cools off.'

'Will you trust me?'

'Why not?'

'Can you believe that it is possible to cross the fifteen feet of hot sand without burning your feet?'

'It seems unlikely.'

'Why not close your eyes for a moment?

Take a few seconds to connect to another part of yourself, notice your breath, how your body relaxes, how the breathing regulates itself, slower and deeper, deeper and slower.

Now, just see yourself crossing the distance, use your imagination, you are crossing the burning sands, yes it is hot, but you can do it, yes, you are doing it, you are doing it and now you are arriving on the other side, entering into the forest, a victory. How does it feel to have mastered this challenge?'

'It feels good, it feels very good.'

'Now you need a mantra.'

'If it's in Sanskrit, it takes me forever to learn.'

'No, nothing so esoteric; just a simple phrase in English. 'I can do it', or something similar will do.'

'There was a story about a little train, that had to rescue some carriages, and pull them up a steep hill, and he kept saying to himself, 'I think I can, I think I can'.'

'That would work very nicely. So, start saying to yourself, 'I think I can, I think I can'.'

'I think I can, I think I can.'

'Good, now again, watch yourself crossing the sand.'
'I think I can, I think I can.'

'Now stand up, keep repeating, keep it up. Good, now, this is not so difficult, I know you can.'

Faron; continuing to chant his mantra, gets up and turns towards the woods.

'Off you go'.

He starts walking, steadily and purposefully, 'I think I can, I think I can,' he can feel the hot sand starting to heat up the sole of a foot, but almost immediately, he follows the step, and it is the other foot in contact, then the other, then the other.

'I think I can, I think I can,' he continues to sing; the cool, quiet woods are closing fast, he is amazed of how quickly … he has arrived.

'I knew I could, I knew I could,' he turns back for the acknowledgement of the other, only to find that the shoreline is again empty of people.

Faron does not really care that much, he did it, he really did it.

The trouble with paradise is that, after a while, it becomes a little repetitive.

Faron, was, after all, a man born in the twentieth century, where survival rhymes with activity and challenge.

Here, other than gathering food and avoiding some dangerous animals and insects, there is nothing to replace the daily challenge of modern life.

So when he hears screams, somewhere off in the distance, he doesn't think twice before grabbing his bow and arrows, and rushing towards the excitement.

One might imagine that Duncan, Jean-Jacques and a woman had been tracking something relatively small, when they must have stumbled on a family of wild boars.

Although in this specific environment, the particularity of these pigs was that they are several orders of magnitude bigger than the biggest of this species that Faron had ever seen.

He is still protected by a screen of trees as he perceives the three tribes' people backed up against a rock-face with two very big and ugly hogs snorting at them, and three, maybe four smaller ones, vaguely circling around.

The human mind is a very unusual type of computer, it takes in the data presented to it and then proceeds to correlate this information with every possible permutation and combination of possibilities and outcomes that can be conceivably related.

The first message that flashes into his mind, is not the most obvious, but just the same, a very important reflection.

If he rescues Duncan, he will either have to return Angelique to him, or fight him for her favours.

Neither outcome seems much to his liking, but the other course of action, or, to be more precise, non-action, to leave them to survive or not, without any intervention from his side, doesn't last long enough in his consciousness to create any real effect.

'Aaaaaaahhhh,' he roars out from his hidden view point. Arrow at the ready, he waits only for one of the adult pigs to turn towards him, to shoot it in the head.

The arrow finds its true mark, and a new species of hideous unicorn is created. It bellows in anger and rage, lowering its head for its massive charge.

Somewhere between a great bull and a four ton haulage truck, the thundering beast charges the small, squat, two legged monkey thing.

Faron knows that he is in real danger; immortal or not, he could be seriously injured, and so experience considerable pain, for quite some weeks, if those vicious tusks should connect to his unprotected skin.

One of natures' little amusing jokes is the attributes of pigs and cows; on first observation, one might very well imagine that these weighty beasts can only be slow and heavy; but as any experienced cowboy can attest, a cow can out-run a horse, and pigs are no slow pokes either.

He is in trouble, and he knows it, he has only the shortest of time to find something to distract it with before it skewers him into a Pierre-Alain-James-Faron-Ferguson-Kebab.

'Olay!' The ballerinic matador presents the bull a false target, stretching out his arms, it follows the action and passes, just inches from his delicate, lithe body.

That the boar would head towards the bow, and ignore Faron, is not logical from a human point of view, but something in the animal's small psyche must count that as just another appendage and hence part of the projected target.

There is activity coming from the direction of the others, his glance sweeps across the scene.

Just long enough to take in that Angelique has arrived, the other hog has reacted to her, while the others are moving in for the attack.

However, his adversary is still in a one to one combat with him, and these are not great odds, when comparing the strength and speed of the combatants.

The bullfighting trick worked well enough that one time, but now he has to find another strategy.

The boar is fast, furious, but not very futé (sly), Faron is quite fast and particularly futé, that should give him the advantage that he needs.

The giant hog has run a little back from the trees, that way it can get up another head of steam, before turning again, back towards the object to be impaled.

Faron slowly backs up, his brown, black eyes fixed on the small, beady black eyes of his enemy.

It stops for a moment, sniffs the air and gets ready to charge.

The man takes another step back, but his path is blocked by one of the enormous trees that fill this ancient forest, he presses himself against the great wood, there is nowhere else to run.

The beast charges; the distance is far from great, in a matter of seconds it is hurtling towards Faron, like a toy attached to an elastic cord, it seems to fly towards its mark.

He doesn't move, she sees what is happening and screams; fear and anguish, an equivalent of 'NO!', but it is much too late to have any effect, the creature is almost upon him.

Its head nods up, this is a reflex reaction so as to force the tusks upwards, with the momentum of the charge, this should be enough to trans-pierce the prey from front to back.

Only he isn't there. In the very last moment, he slides round the tree, just avoiding the sharp edge of the left tusk.

The boar, for its part, can do nothing to avoid the tree, it enters into it with all its might and force, the bark splits and the horns enter, it can neither advance nor retreat.

It squeals in anger, frustration, then in pain, as the hunting party quickly dispatch it, and then it is all over.

18. One's just reward

They are back in the camp; it is another feast, two great, wild boars to eat now and four little ones captured and penned up, there is good reason to celebrate.

Faron is happy in the expectation to taste meat again, neither he nor Angelique were very successful at hunting or trapping, but he cannot relax, how can he, when he knows not how Duncan will punish him for running off with his woman.

As is his role, Duncan is cutting the first portions of the meat off the roasting carcass; he digs in with his sharp stone and cuts out the heart. Pulling it up and out, he looks round for something or someone.

'Faan', he shouts, and again, 'Faan', Angelique appears from somewhere, grabs him by the arm and drags him towards Duncan. Faron is too surprised to resist,

'Faan', Duncan turns to him and offers him the heart.

'Why so I do, the noblest that I have.'

'Faan', he gives the prize to Faron, who smiles and takes it, still bewildered, but incredibly relieved by this gesture of fraternity.

'You see, survival, is not every man for himself, or the survival of the fittest. Survival is a group concern; if your group, tribe, team do well, then you can also do well.'

'Survival is for team players.'

'There, now you've got it.'

'But do you think that it will be okay if Angelique stays with me?'

'Oh, you might do even better than her.'

'What do you mean?'

'Come, and I will show you.' He takes Faron by the hand and leads him into the darkness behind one of the huts. As they come out …

'Careful, you don't want to fall into a canal.'

'Canal?'

'Yes, Venice is full of them …'

The Island of Serenity
Book 2

Sun & Rain:

Pierre Alain and Angelique become friends, which is fine for them, but not at all acceptable to his parents, who use their considerable means to keep the two young hearts separated.

Pierre Alain is sent off to boarding school, where he meets up with his two future, best friends; Duncan and Mike

His parents attempts to keep the two lovers apart is to no avail, it seems that fate has other plans that no-one is capable to thwart.

The Island of Serenity
Book 3

Pleasure

Vol 1

Pt 1

Faron finds himself in a past version of Venice, as the owner of an old but grand hotel that doubles as meeting place for the wealthy men of the City and the high class escort girls that live in the establishment.

Faron can do anything that he likes without limitation or cost. Not only can he avail himself of the girls, but can eat and drink, without limit, but never suffer from a hangover, nor gain a gram.

So why has the enigmatic guide brought him here, and will his limitless access to life's offerings really bring him the pleasure that he is destined to experience?

Pt 2

Faron arrives in a dream of modern day Venice, only here his guide takes him into the secret, inner world of women.

The Island of Serenity
Book 3

Pleasure
Vol 2

Pt 1
Faron's quest to find his ability to experience pleasure leads him to an Ancient Chinese Geisha house, where he must first learn how to pleasure others.

Pt2
The final part of Faron's quest to experience pleasure takes him to the exotic sights, tastes and smells of a modern day Indian.

What experiences and adventures has his guide got in store for him, so that eventually he will realise that it is now time to learn the painful lessons of pleasure.

Tasty Bites

(Series – published or in preproduction)

Face to Face

A young teacher asks to befriend an older colleague on Face Book, "I have a very delicate situation, for which I would appreciate your advice"

Free 2 Luv

The e-mail exchanges between; RichBitch, SecretLover, the mother, the bestie, and the lawyer, expose a complicated and surprising story

Heresy

An e-mail from a future controlled by the major pharmaceutical companies, "please do what you can to change this situation, now, before it happens ...

Love you to death

A toy town parable, populated by your favourite playthings, about the dangerous game of dependency and co-dependency

Master of all Masters

In an ancient land, the disciples argue about who is the Master of all Masters. The solution is to create a competition

Pandora's Box

If you had a magic box, into which you could bury all your negative thoughts and feelings, wouldn't that be wonderful?

Shame of a family	Being born different can be a heavy burden to bear. Especially for the family
The Noble Princess	If you were just a humble Saxon, would you be good enough to marry a noble Norman Princess?
The Ugly Barren Fruit Tree	A weird foreign tree that bears no fruit, in an apple orchard. What value can it possibly have?
The Woman of my Dreams	What would you do, if the woman that you fell in love with in your dream, suddenly appears in real life?

None Fiction:

The Zen approach to Low Impact Training and Sports
A simple method for achieving a healthy body and a healthy mind

Many of us approach our fitness and sports activities in an aggressive and competitive fashion.

And even if we feel that we succeed to break out of our comfort zones and win against ourselves or our opponent, there is an important cost to bear.

This level of violence that we have come to accept, so as to reach our goals is also an aggression against ourselves. By removing this need to 'win at any price', and tuning in with our bodies and emotions, we can achieve an enormous amount, all the while being in harmony with our mind, body and spirit.

The Zen approach to Low Impact Training and Sports, is a new softer approach where you can have the best of all worlds.

Adventures with the Master

Dhargey was a sickly child or so his parents treated him.
He was too weak to join the army or work in the fields or even join the
monastery as a normal trainee monk.

To explain to the 'Young Master' why he should be accepted into the order
with a lightened program, he was forced to accompany the revered old man a
little ways up the mountain.

As his parents watched him leave; somewhere they felt that they would never
see their sickly, fragile boy ever again, somewhere they were totally right.

He was a happy, healthy seven year old until he witnessed the riders, dressed
in red and black, destroying his village and murdering his parents; the trauma
cut deep into his psyche.

Only the chance meeting with a wandering monk could set him back onto the
road towards health and serenity.

Through meditation, initiations, stories, taming wild horses, becoming a
monkey, mastering the staff and the sword; the future 'Young Master'
prepares to face his greatest demon.

Two men, two journeys, one goal.

THE TALES OF
PETER THE PIXIE

Peter the innocent, honest, young pixie, and his friends; Elli, the, 'much older then she looks', modest but powerful Fairy, Timothy, the old, trustworthy, Toad and the, ever so noble, Fire Dragon, are the best of friends.

Together, they experience many wonderful and heart-warming adventures.

Told in a classical children's story style; Peter and his friends, meet all kinds of creatures and situations.

As with all children, Peter is often confronted with experiences that he does not know how best to deal with, and he often reacts in ways that are not the most appropriate. Fortunately; with the help of his good friends, good will and common sense, everything always turns out for the best.

Picturing the Mind

A simple, single model, accessible to everyone, to explain the development, functioning and dis-functioning of the human psyche.

Abstract:

For the common man and woman in the street, the complex and competing theories and models of the human psyche; its development, functioning and dis-functioning are often unhelpful for their understanding of themselves.

This becomes even more problematic when they find themselves in difficulty, as often, even the mental health professionals, who are experts in their own fields, find themselves at a loss to communicate successfully how and why the patent is unwell and what needs to happen to find or regain a healthy balance.

This opens up the question; 'is it possible to image a simple, single model, accessible to everyone, to explain the development, functioning and dis-functioning of the human psyche?'

One that builds on existing theories and models, benefitting from the mass of experience and research of 'modern western' psychological concepts and ideas, but also integrating traditional visions of the human psyche and modern theories from the physical sciences.

Picturing the Mind, is an attempt to answer to this need.

REMEMBER
Stories and poems for self-help and self-development based on
techniques of Ericksonian and auto-hypnosis

*Dusk falls, the world shrinks little by little into a smaller and smaller circle
as the light continues to diminish.*
*The centre of this world is illuminated by a small, crackling sun; the flames
dance, and the rough faces of the people gathered there are lit by the fire of
their expectations.*
*The old man will begin to speak, he will explain to them how the world is,
how it was, how it was created. He will help them understand how things
have a sense, an order, a way that they need to be.*
*He will clarify the sources of un-wellness and unhappiness, what is sickness,
where it comes from, how to notice it and... how to heal it.*
*To heal the sick, he will call forth the forces of the invisible realms, maybe
he will sing, certainly he will talk, and talk, and talk.*

Since the beginning of time we have gathered round those who can bring
us the answers to our questions and the means to alleviate our sufferings.
This practice has not fundamentally changed since the earliest times; in
every era, continent and culture we have found and continue to find these
experiences.

In this, amongst the oldest of the healing traditions, he has succeeded to meld
modern therapy theories and techniques with stories and poems of the highest
quality.

With much humanity, clinical vignettes, common sense and lots of humour,
the reader is gently carried from situation to situation. Whether the problems
described concern you directly, indirectly or not at all, you will surely find
interest and benefits from the wealth of insights and advices contained within
and the conscious or unconscious positive changes through reading the stories
and poems.

CPSIA information can be obtained
at www.ICGtesting.com
Printed in the USA
BVHW092150290922
648371BV00011B/72